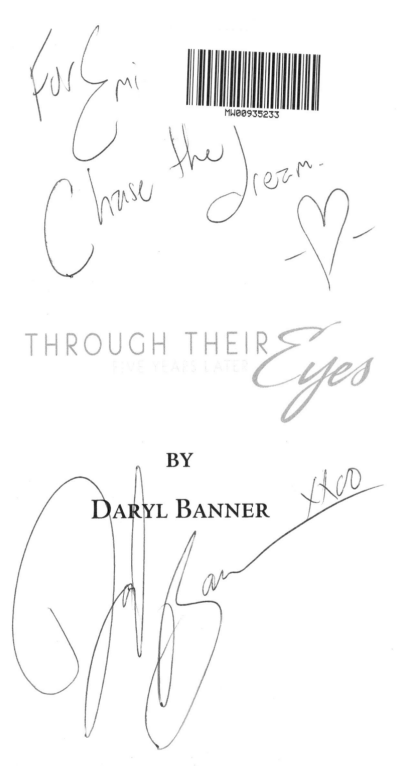

For Emi

Chase the dream. ♡

THROUGH THEIR Eyes
FIVE YEARS LATER

BY

DARYL BANNER

xxoo

Through Their Eyes: Five Years Later
A College Obsession Romance Novella

Cover Models : Nathan Hainline & Cassady Rose
Cover Photographer : Nathan Hainline
Cover Design : Daryl Banner
Interior Design : Daryl Banner

Images on the back cover are from the original covers of
Read My Lips, Beneath The Skin, & With These Hands,
designed by Kari Ayasha.

Other books by Daryl Banner

List of Chapters

Author's Note

The events that take place in this sequel novella follow up with all of our couples five years after the end of the College Obsession Romance Series. To avoid spoilers, I strongly recommend that you read the main series first: *Read My Lips, Beneath The Skin, & With These Hands.*

Thank you for joining me during these sexy, fun, and sometimes *tumultuous* years at Klangburg University. I truly hope through the eyes of Dessie, Clayton, Brant, Nell, Sam, Dmitri, and the rest of their friends, that you felt the love ... and maybe discovered a thing or two along the way.

Peace and love
    and happy reading always,
        Daryl

Brant

– Five Years Later –

A four-year-old cackles maniacally as she tears across the room clutching a TV remote. A worn-out, pregnant Nell in sweats shouts out after her from the couch, while our twin two-year-old girls on the floor nearby are apparently trying to out-scream one another.

Ever since I was a kid, I always wished I'd grow up to be surrounded by pretty girls.

Maybe I should've been more specific.

My mother calls out from the kitchen asking if we need an exorcist, to which my dad lets out a hearty guffaw from upstairs. Our family dog, a pretty black female Scottish Terrier named Pandora, tears across the room after our four-year-old, panting and barking and panting some more.

This is normal. Don't worry. No one's being chased by a machete-wielding murderer, despite how it may appear.

On our four-year-old's fourth lap around the room, I swipe her right off her feet and bring her up to my face. "Zara," I scold lovingly after giving her a kiss on the cheek. "You know your mommy and I love you ever so dearly, right?"

To that, little Zara just brings the remote to her mouth and giggles, then sheepishly nods. Her tiny squeezing fingers change the TV channel to Discovery.

"So why in the world are you actin' like you've been possessed by spirits of the wild? You're runnin' around here scaring your sisters."

"I don't know." She bites the remote. The channel changes to MTV.

"Please hand me the remote, sweetie."

"No."

I set her down, then crouch down to bring my eyes level with hers. "You know, someday sooner than you realize, you're gonna be the big lady of the house. Your little sisters are going to look up to you. You want to be a good older sister, don't you?"

Zara's face scrunches up. "I'm not old!" She put some fingers in my face. "I'm only this many!"

"And that includes being a good sister to your

new little brother," I go on, pointing at Nell's belly.

"It could be another girl," throws in Nell with a dark smirk. "Don't count your blessings just yet."

"I'll hear none of that," I retort back to her playfully, then return my stern gaze to Zara. "That's a lot of responsibility for a little girl, Zara, I know. But part of being a good *totally-not-old* big sister ... is knowing *not* to steal the remote while everyone else is watching Nickelodeon."

"It's *Jersey Shore* now," mumbles Nell.

I give one of Zara's black curls of hair a playful flick, inspiring another giggle. "Please hand me the remote before you and your dear sisters start seeing things you're not supposed to see for another ten years."

"No."

"I didn't even know they still ran re-runs of this show," grumbles Nell, her face scrunched up.

"Ooh, I like the one with the abs!" my mother calls out from the kitchen.

I wiggle my fingers. "Remote, Zara, before we have ourselves a situation."

"There's a *situation* on TV already," shouts Nell.

"Ooh, the abs guy!" announces my mother at the kitchen doorway, a half-cleaned frying pan in her hand from the breakfast feast we just had.

I ignore my mother and my beautiful wife. "Zara. You wanna be a good girl, right?"

"No."

I know she's just playing with me, but I bite my lip and think about what will really convince her. Then I change my tack entirely. "You know, when we get to New York, only good girls and boys are allowed to have a tasty piece of Aunt Dessie's triple chocolate cake."

Zara's eyes grow double. Her lips quiver.

"Though, to be fair, it's not really Aunt *Dessie's* cake, per se. It's cake her mother's infamous live-in chef makes, but it's pretty much the stuff of hot, melty chocolate dreams."

"Chocolate dreams?" moans Zara, dreaming it.

I lick my lips. "I can taste it now if I close my eyes ..."

"I want a piece!" she cries out.

"Hmm." I pretend to consider it, probably for too long a time to not be considered child cruelty. I mean, cake is a *very* serious matter. "I'm not so sure, Zara. I mean, only *good* girls and boys are allowed a piece of the succulent, delicious cake, and since you're holding the remote hostage—"

The remote slaps my palm the next second. It's followed by a scowl on Zara's adorable little face that matches Nell's so well, it breaks my heart. She's such a fireball and always has been since birth. Someday, she's going to ignite the world.

But before that happens, I simply mend the situation by swinging her up into my arms, tossing the remote to Nell, and showering my daughter's face with an abundance of wet, slobbery kisses, which earns a whole new explosion of giggles and squeals of protest.

Yeah, gross. I know. I'm one of those daddy's-girl kind of daddies now.

And it's my new favorite thing.

Time flies by so fast, I'm in the kitchen hugging my parents goodbye already. "It's just for the weekend. As long as the twins have their Batty and Lady, they'll be happy."

"Oh, don't worry about it." My mother gives me a wink and a nudge, then eyes the twins who are gathered up in my dad's arms. "They'll be just fine with us. But are you sure Nell is up for the trip?"

"Yeah, she said she's excited to see New York."

"Pack some crackers in her purse. Or maybe something for the plane in case she gets …" My mom makes a gesture at her belly. "Morning sickness was bad her last pregnancy, too."

"I remember. We'll grab something from the pantry before we head out. Pad our luggage with snacks too, just in case."

"I worry about her making this big trip." My mom wrings her hands and stares off at the other room where Nell and Zara are on the couch.

"We'll be fine."

"Another on the way," my mom mumbles on, her tone turning sassy, "and then what, you big baby-maker you? Yet another?"

"We're stopping after this one."

She narrows her eyes. "You said that after the twins."

"But we mean it this time."

"Even if it's another girl?"

"It's going to be a boy."

My mom shakes her head. "Brant, you need to get yourself *clipped*. Overpopulation is a serious issue in this world."

My father, still holding our two-year-olds, gives one a squeeze in his left arm while planting a kiss on the forehead of the other, then nods at me. "You should let us watch your girls more often."

I chuckle at him. "If you can tell the twins apart by now, then you're more than welcome."

The truth is, the twins couldn't be more different. Little Dalia is clutching Batty, her furry black bat with white squishy fangs, while Eden hugs her favorite doll to her chest—a Disney princess whose real name has been traded for what Eden prefers to call her: Lady. I love my twins to death, but I won't lie, there have been a few times in the beginning when I called one by the other's name. I'm not proud of it. But then Dalia started taking an unnatural liking to skulls and furry black bats (seriously, just seeing one makes her giggle), and Eden gravitated towards green dresses and rebellious Disney princesses. Now they look like mirror images of one another—the wicked and the dainty. They both look exactly like Nell, though maybe they have my eyes.

"You packed that new jacket I got Zara, right?"

"Oh, that big puffy thing? Of course." I wink at my mother. "I wouldn't let my little girl experience the New York December frigidness without being properly armored."

"Ooh! You might even see *snow*!" She smiles wistfully, gives my shirt a tug, then pats me on the cheek. "You all should probably get going. The traffic is going to be nuts tonight."

My chest flutters with a bit of anxiousness. It's like I keep forgetting where we're about to head off to and why. "Nell and I were idiots planning this trip so last minute, huh?"

"And with Christmas just a few weeks away? You'll be lucky to even get there at all. If you don't make it in time, can't Clayton change your tickets to tomorrow, or—?"

"No, no. They don't know. That's the whole thing. It's a *surprise*. Orchestrated by Sam, of all people," I add with a nervous chuckle. "Of course, it also isn't too late to cancel, especially since I—"

"You declined the last three times they invited you to New York," my dad reminds me with a lift of an eyebrow, lightly bouncing the twins in his arms. "If I didn't know better, I'd say you were avoiding seeing them at all."

"I'm not *avoiding* them," I retort too quickly. "I'm just ... It was just ..."

"Your babies," my mom answers for me, saving me the trouble. "You and Nell popped them out back to back with already another on the way. Really, do Clayton and his wife seriously expect you to just drop everything and run up to New York every time they have a new show debuting? It's not like *they* have any little ones, otherwise they might actually understand what it's like."

I can tell my mom is getting a touch heated—as this is a hot button for her—so I step in and give her back a quick rub. "Nah, I doubt they blame us. Clayboy is super happy that we're building a family. He's especially excited that we did the whole sign language thing with Zara. She can't wait to show off her super skills in person. Skype and FaceTime just don't do her cuteness justice."

My mom's face softens, but only a touch. "Someday, Clayton is going to realize the man you've grown into. They need to take you more seriously, he and his wife. You're not the boy who plays video games until sunrise and takes a different girl to every school dance anymore."

I catch sight of Nell in the other room talking to Zara on her lap, the pair of them looking like they just recovered from laughing at some joke. It seems like just yesterday that I was posing naked in her art class, showing off my junk to a room full of strangers. It was the best day of my life, the day I risked it all just to get a flicker of attention from that hot chick with the black hair and the dark, up-to-no-good glint in her eyes.

"Nope," I agree, still watching Nell. "Definitely not that boy anymore."

Then my mom pulls me into the tightest hug I've felt in years, and over the sound of laughter and whatever's mumbling on the TV, I tell my mom I love her and wish her the best of luck with my twin demon spawn, which she will need.

Soon, I'm sitting on a bench in the airport next to the love of my life, and we're waiting on our flight. Zara sits in the chair next to me swinging her feet like axe-wielding pendulums. Nell hugs a bag to her chest, her lips pursed in thought as she stares across the hum of the enormous crowded room.

I guess I'm lost in a few thoughts myself as I watch the side of her face. A thought cuts into the general murmur. "Nell, did you remember the—?"

"Yes," she cuts me off with a crooked smile. "And the champagne bottle. And the gift for Sam and Dmitri, our generous hosts."

"And the crackers I packed in your purse for you."

"Yep. Just in case our unborn daughter gives me the delightful sensation of wanting to hurl."

"Or unborn son."

"Likely daughter." She smirks at me. "Relax, Brant. I'm fine. It's even so early, yet. I'm not even showing."

I nod, then take a deep breath. "Sorry, I'm ..." I let out a short burst of air. "I don't know what I am."

"It's been a long time since you've seen Clayton," Nell points out. "Over a year, hasn't it been?"

I bite my lip and shrug. I'd lie if I said I hadn't given it a lot of thought. In truth, it's all I've been thinking about for the past week. Clayton and I grew up together. We used to be the best of friends, and nothing short of a category ten hurricane could separate us. Then that category ten hurricane came in the form of a talented, special young woman named Dessie who stole his dark little heart, and they have been inseparable ever since. I'm happy for him—really, I am—but there are many times when I find myself missing my best friend. We text each other fairly often, but it doesn't compare to how things used to be. The fact is, I miss seeing his stupid face. I miss his dumb jokes that used to make me laugh so hard, I'd snort Dr. Pepper out of my flared nostrils. I miss fumbling with my hands before I produced an actual sign that his deaf ass could understand. I regret never having given a genuine effort to learning sign language so that I could really talk to my best friend the way our old roommate and buddy Dmitri can. *Shit, I'll be seeing Dmitri again, too—staying at his and Sam's place, no less.*

"Don't let it get to you," Nell whispers to me. "He's going to be happy as shit to see your face. Even if you turned down his offers to visit him a hundred times."

"Why doesn't *his* ass come down to *Texas*?" I argue, feeling a pinch of the frustration my mom was trying to express in the kitchen before we left. "He knows I have a family now. He knows it isn't easy for me to—"

"Brant. Stop. It's okay. I seriously doubt he blames you."

"Maybe." My leg bounces in place as I pick at my cuticles, staring down at my lap.

Nell keeps fishing. "Is it ... the whole surprise thing that's got your head in a mess?"

"I'm not ... *in a mess.*" I smirk, abandon my half-picked fingers, and turn my head to my loving wife. "Listen, though I'd be lying if I didn't say that staying with Sam and Dmitri is ... a little weird ..."

"We could've gotten a nice hotel room."

"Yeah. And, I mean, I used to share a place with the D-man, but still ..."

"It's been a long while," she finishes for me.

"Long while," I agree.

"You're afraid they've changed. That you'll have nothing to talk about."

"Except for his porn collection. Which I'm sure Sam has become all the more familiar with over the years." I laugh at that suddenly, some random memory resurfacing when I teased Dmitri about his jerking addiction and how kinky Sam probably is underneath all the deadpan demeanor. "Maybe I'm just worried for nothing."

"You get it from your mother."

The loud speaker calls for a flight, announcing that the plane is ready to board. Nell and I glance up, listening, until we realize it's another flight and not our own that's ready.

Nell sighs and puts a hand over mine. "I hate flying. Did I mention that? Hate, hate, hate, *hate* flying."

"Just think of it as a magical chair in the sky encased by a lot of metal and the smiling faces of uniformed flight attendants who ensure that we are comfortable," I suggest with a flashy grin.

"That doesn't help."

"I packed crackers."

"*I know.*"

I glance over at Zara, who has apparently taken to counting the people sitting in the row of chairs across from us. If I didn't know better, I'd think Zara was two steps away from becoming a math prodigy. I can already picture her talking back to her teacher on the first day of kindergarten and sassily announcing that she already knows her multiplication tables by the first grade.

That Zara is going places.

"I can't wait for Clayton to get stampeded by his most ferocious goddaughter," I throw back with a chuckle. "And it's going to be very amusing for me. Maybe for Dessie, too."

"Definitely for me," mutters Nell. Her phone is in her hand in the next instant, typing away one-handed.

My fingers run up Nell's long neck, tangling themselves in her dark hair. "I'm the first of the whole gang to knock up my wife. Three times in a row, at that." Nell swats my arm, but doesn't pull away from the tease and tickle of my fingers in her hair. I laugh. "Hey, it's true. Can't deny the facts."

"Can't blame Dessie, really." Nell puts away her phone, bored with it already, and turns her head, her dark eyes flashing and her lips pulling up at one corner. "It ... can't be easy for a world-traveling performer and songstress like her to go through a pregnancy, not with all the touring and contracts she has to sign to be cast in her big Broadway shows and what-have-you. She's got quite the actor's life, that Desdemona Lebeau-Watts."

"Still not used to that hyphenated last name." I keep dragging my hand through her hair, then find myself pulling her head toward mine. "You look so beautiful, Nell *Rudawski*."

"Stop it."

"I gotta say it over and over. It still feels so new to me. You're mine, Mrs. Rudawski."

"Oh, great. I'm like a trophy, now."

"Better that than an art exhibit tied to a platform on display for the world to see," I tease, recalling a particular day where that very thing was done to me—by Nell, no less.

She smirks, remembering. "You looked sexy in those tiny black briefs."

"You look sexy in anything." My hand still strokes her soft hair. "Just as beautiful as the day I met you."

Nell faces me completely, then brings her lips halfway to mine. Before our lips have a chance to meet, she stops and eyes me. "You're deflecting with sex again."

I flinch. "Hmm?"

"You know you do this, right? When you're nervous. Or upset. Or bothered ... *perturbed* by a conundrum you can't quite figure out. Your mind goes straight to sex." She tilts her head, all her hair swishing to one side. "Tell me I'm wrong."

The words clog up my throat, none of them spilling out. I catch myself staring at her beautiful face with my lips hanging open, unable to refute her.

"See?" Then she gives my lips a kiss—more of a peck, really—and draws back. "You just need to relax, Brant. Clayton is going to admire all the hard work you've put into this family. Not to mention your photography."

"Nell ..."

"You know I'm right. Dmitri is going to be *thrilled* to see Zara. And Sam ... well, Sam's Sam. Not much to say about that."

That gets a genuine smile from me. "Sam's Sam," I agree. "She'll probably comment on my hair. It's a lot shaggier than the last time they've all seen me."

Now it's Nell's turn to bring a hand up to my head, threading her fingers in my medium-length tangles of brown knots and wavy strands. "You've skipped a haircut or two or seven, that's for sure."

"Blame my shaggy mess on the twins." I eye Nell. "Can we please pray for a boy? That's all I ask. Just one son. Please."

"So we can have your player genes pass on to a poor, unsuspecting and oddly overconfident boy who is way too good-looking, drives all the girls wild, and gets into constant trouble?"

I smirk cockily. "So you're saying I'm way too good-looking and drive you wild?"

Nell pinches my nose, inspiring a scoff and a chortle from me. "*And get into constant trouble.* Face it: a son would *destroy* this family. Let's be real, Brant. You and I are best at raising an army of strong-willed young women."

"Like *you*."

She shrugs and tosses her hair. "Better than me.

Much, much better than me."

I put a kiss right on her soft, plush lips. "I love you so damned much, babe."

"Right back at you." Then she returns the kiss, and our lips don't separate. The loud speaker throws words over our heads, and it isn't until the second time they're called out that we realize they're meant for us. Our flight is boarding.

It's time.

Dessie

I take a deep, deep breath. It's the kind of breath where I can feel every inch of my lungs expand, almost to the point of bursting. Then when I let it all out, it's like I'm weightless and nothing exists at all in the world but my skeleton and my skin.

And my makeup sponges. "I don't know why I'm so nervous," I mumble into the blindingly-lit mirror.

Victoria, who's been my rock since the day we lived in dorms across the hall from one another so many years ago, looks at me through the reflection in the mirror. "You got this, girl."

"Do I?" I shake my head. "I can't help but constantly fight the feeling that I only have this show and this ... this *opportunity* because of my family's prestige. It feels unearned. I'm opening a show on Broadway. *Broadway* for fuck's sake."

"Are you kidding me right now?" Victoria leans

toward the mirror, preferring to speak to my reflection instead of me directly. Oddly, it's far more effective, as it freezes my act of applying makeup to my face. "You totally deserve this, Desdemona. Don't you dare discount how many hours, days, months, and *years* of sweat it's taken to get to this point."

"Uh-oh. You're using my full name," I note with mock wariness. "You mean business."

Victoria narrows her eyes. "You have worked your skinny little tushie off since the day I met you. You have more talent in your *thumb* than I have in my whole body."

I eye her hard. "Okay, *that's* not true, miss award-winning costume designer."

She breaks her stern character for a second to put a hand to her chest and bat her eyelashes. "Now, now. Tonight is your night to shine the spotlight on sharp writing, witty lyrics, and music that is as viscerally cutting as it is soulful. Not *my* night to shine with my whimsical-yet-totally-relatable costume design."

"You know I love you, right?"

"My point is that this is not a fluke, or an act of a string-pulling, or an undeserved thing." Victoria turns away from the mirror and faces me head-on now, pulling my face toward hers. "And when that audience out there hears your music ..."

"And sees *your* amazing costumes."

"And sees it all lit up beautifully and cleverly by your brooding block of meat that is Clayton," she adds, inspiring a short and teary laugh from me, "they will know that they are seeing real art, and they will be moved."

"The day I first saw Clayton is the same day you and I met," I note, feeling oddly nostalgic.

"And Eric. And Chloe. What's your point? Listen." She leans in closer. "Those people out there in the audience, they are *thrilled* to see your work. I promise you, they *will* be talking about your show all the way to dinner, discussing the nuances of your plot and your characters, and humming the tunes over caviar and buttered lobster tails."

I bite my lip. "Did you *have* to say that? I haven't eaten as much a block of *cheese* since noon."

Victoria laughs, then picks up a brush and starts to work out the last remaining knots in my annoyingly long hair. "Don't worry. You'll have plenty of delicacies *and then some* to gobble down at the after party."

"Can we cancel that?"

"Oh, and send all eighty of your high-profile guests and their plus-ones off to figure out new plans for tonight? Good idea. They didn't already reconfigure their schedules to allot for their family seeing the premiere of a brand new dramedy musical about life and death. They didn't already tell their kids to fuck off and sleep well with the overpriced nanny looking over their big, tall townhouses."

I roll my eyes. "Thanks for the perspective."

"Hey. People need something to do. Your audience will be packed from one end to the other no matter when you chose to debut. And with the subject matter, I think it's perfect. Broadway never sleeps anyway."

"Broadway never sleeps," I agree, suddenly thinking about how little I slept last night. I've never been this anxious about a show opening. Or maybe late night's lack of sleep was due to Clayton's beastly snoring. Seriously, he vibrated the whole bed and stayed pressed up against me the entire night with me trapped in his arms. I couldn't get away if I tried.

And under normal circumstances, that's basically the definition of my happily-ever after: getting the pleasure of being trapped in my man's muscular, tatted arms every night, safe as an oatmeal raisin cookie on a plate of chocolate chip cookies. (Seriously, who goes for the oatmeal raisin cookies when you have the choice of classic-and-delectable chocolate chip?)

There is, however, nothing *normal* about Clayton's snoring.

Now, I have no more than an hour—maybe two—of sleep to run on. My show is debuting. Then I have a ritzy, upscale after party to contend with. All of Broadway's biggest stars, directors, and their spouses (or boy toys) will be there. Why can't I just have a little intimate gathering with my modest handful of best friends? Give me Sam, Victoria, and my husband Clayton, then cast away the rest of the world.

Well, I guess we'd need Dmitri in there, since he's besties with Clayton and is sorta Sam's love bird and lifetime companion, even if they still boldly reject the institution of marriage outright.

Oh, and Victoria's guy Dirk, who is basically a rocker and a sonic poet and will probably propose to her any day now.

Oh, and Eric, who is tragically dependent on Dmitri's artistic opinion on *everything*, even though we constantly tell him how brilliant his script-writing skills are. Also, he always brings a bottle of wine or champagne no matter what the occasion is. (Thank God he gave up his illegal homebrewed cat pee side business.)

And I guess that means we need to add Bailey to my hypothetical party too, Eric's boyfriend who finally made the move to New York last year after four years of tortured commuting and long distance Skyping—though he's also since become possessive and never lets Eric do anything on his own anymore, let alone come to the opening of my show.

And maybe we'll have to pull Chloe into our gathering too, if it's one of her weekends where she's actually here working in New York instead of Los Angeles.

Yikes. I guess my tiny circle of friends has grown considerably since the Klangburg days.

But what about Brant and Nell ...?

"Aces Play is going to be here before we know it," Victoria warns me, stirring me from my thoughts.

Places is what's typically called out when it's time for the actors to get in place for the start of a show. Ever since a few years after college, Victoria and I have taken up to saying it in Pig Latin— *acesplay.* It's kind of our thing.

"I was just thinking about Brant and Nell," I confess as I resume putting on my makeup. "Clayton hasn't seen them in a long time. I know they're busy with all their little ones, but—"

"Oh, I'm sure you all will crash back together eventually. You can pull the Clayton out of Texas, but you can't pull the ... the Brant out of ... the ..." Victoria shakes her head. "I couldn't make the saying work. Ignore me. I'm drunk."

"Dang it, Victoria. You weren't allowed to drink before act two!" I tease, swatting her with my makeup brush. "Now I feel left out!"

"I'll get you liquored up for tonight. No worries."

I laugh at that, then resume putting on my makeup. My mind goes right back to Clayton and his estranged best friend. Something about it is bothering me. "Do you think—?"

"What?"

The last swab of foundation is pressed onto my

forehead, then I set the sponge down and stare at my array of rouges and highlights and lowlights as if I don't recognize them. "Do you think ... Clayton resents me?"

Victoria's eyes flash in the mirror. "Why the heck would you ask something ridiculous like that?"

"For taking him away from his best friend," I clarify. "For making him move all the way up here to New York with me, transplanting his whole life. For ..." I sigh, my hand suddenly finding itself on my belly, as if my body has teamed up with my subconscious, directing my mind right to my deepest fear. "For denying him ... a family."

"Dessie."

I keep going. "I think about Brant and Nell and how they have all these children ..."

"Have you *met* Brant and Nell?" she fires back, quirking an eyebrow. "They're, like, sex monster one and sex monster two. They're going to have fifteen children before we get another president."

"And then I look at *us*, and ... well, let's face it, we're not getting any younger."

"Unlike any of the rest of us, you have a career that literally requires your body. You don't have the same liberties to do as you please like the others have. Clayton is behind you one hundred percent. Think about it. If you two want to start a family, you'll do it when it's the right time."

I let out a sigh, then choose a lowlight and dab a brush into it. I stare at my face, deciding where to apply it. "What if it's never right?"

Victoria shrugs. "Then it's never right. There are tons of couples out there who don't have children."

"Clayton would make such a great father."

"I doubt Dirk and I would ever consider kids, to be honest. He's got a life on the road with his two-man band. I've got my fabrics and questionable design choices."

I chuckle dryly at that, shadowing the hollows of my cheeks. "I like your design choices." I freeze suddenly. "Wait. That's *Sam's* story."

"Come again?"

"Her dad's a traveling musician. Her mom travels with him. If they had hit the road way back when and never settled to have a kid ... Sam wouldn't exist. Our Sam."

"You're overthinking this. Stop."

"What if my selfishness is preventing my *own* Sam from existing?" I gape and turn to my friend. "I could have a little Sam in this world."

Victoria grabs my hands and gives them a gentle shake. "You're swimming in your own head now, girl. And it's all because of your show. You're nervous, but there's no reason to be, because they are going to love your show. You're just channeling your character. Life ... Death ... a baby ..."

"You think this is just stage fright?"

"No." She winks. "You're just getting into character."

After a moment, I let myself smile and try to let in whatever little bit of relief I can. Or maybe it's more of a letting *out* that I'm trying to accomplish. I have so many worries playing tennis in my head, but I don't know which one to track with my eyes and which one to put into words. Should I just let them bounce around until they shrink down to nothing? Should I let them all out on stage in subliminal bursts of emotion?

Is Clayton truly happy with this life we've built here together? *Or is there something missing ...?*

Dmitri

Brant and Nell arrived at our place half an hour ago, and already Sam and Nell are lost in conversation about some TV show they both watch about unsolved murders, analyzing a recent episode piece by piece, scene by scene, character by mysterious character.

And I'm trapped in a prison of my own "mysterious" characters. I'm stuck—creatively, literarily, emotionally—and I can't seem to find a way out. It's like a maze in my mind that is equal parts bursting inspiration as well as deflating, crippling self-doubt.

"Dude. You haven't aged a day."

I flinch and turn to Brant, who's helped himself to a beer from my fridge. "You look like you've aged approximately five years," I shoot right back, feeling sassy.

Brant finds that way too funny, snorting over the mouth of his beer bottle and cackling with his eyes squeezed shut. For a second, it's just like the old days when we'd kick back on the couch of our old apartment—Eric or Clayton there with us—and we're laughing away the hours over bottles or cans of beer and a video game.

"Careful," I add with a nod at the bottle. "Drink too many of those, you'll exchange that six-pack you have for the one in my fridge."

"The only ones that matter come in twelve-packs, my friend." Brant winks, then punches me in the shoulder as he comes to lean on the kitchen counter next to me. "It's the kids, man. They got me whipped. Ain't easy raising three girls."

"I can't even begin to imagine," I confess, staring over the counter at Nell and Sam as they keep going on about their favorite show. Brant's little four-year-old Zara sits between them keeping herself occupied with a picture book full of mythological creatures Sam and I gave her. I can see the Pegasus on the cover from here.

"I sometimes envy you and Sam and Clayton and Dessie ... this life you have up here ... but then I remember how fucking cold it gets."

I groan. "No kidding. I'm still not used to it."

"And it's supposed to snow tomorrow?" asks

Brant, his face wrinkled. "Really? This Texan here is supposed to somehow survive that shit?"

"Hope you packed jackets."

"Of course we did. This thirty degree shit you got going tonight, I'm gonna be bundled up like that kid from *A Christmas Story*. Won't be able to bend my damned arms."

I smile and fold my arms. "It's gonna drop to below twenty in a matter of hours."

"Fuck me."

The pair of us continue watching Nell and Sam for a minute or two, during which the characters in my head cross their arms defiantly and glare at one another from across a shapeless, undefined waiting room of sorts. I swear, writer's block is the worst. There is nothing more I desire in this wretched world than to let out this alleged masterpiece from my mind and weave the perfect story into existence before my eyes ... and yet I sit in front of the computer and nothing comes. It's like my characters are all pissed at each other and no one wants to talk.

I'm about to employ torture techniques on all of them, determined to make them speak. *Tell me your stories!* I'd demand of them. *Tell me what's in your heads so I can get you out of mine!*

"You ever miss Klangburg?"

His question catches me off-guard. "I was just thinking about it a couple days ago," I admit. "Some of my classes. Some of the professors. The freedom. The campus. *Throng & Song*. Dessie's weird, super emo songs she'd put on there. Yeah, I miss it."

Brant smiles and kicks back his beer, then sets it on the counter and bats it back and forth between his rough palms. "Yeah, me too. Was thinking I might go back and actually, like, finish my degree."

"Mister Drop-Out is going back, huh?" I laugh at the idea of a five-years-older Brant strutting across the campus like he still owns it. "And who's gonna raise your daughters while you're busy cradle-robbing?"

Brant wipes his face with a hand, then shakes his head. "It's great to see you still think so highly of me."

I chuckle. "To be fair, you *have* changed quite a bit. You know I'm teasing."

"Sure, sure. Everyone's teasing." Brant throws me a look, then elbows my ribs. "They *do* offer online classes, you know. I *can* do it and still keep my photography gig up. Oh, and Nell's got this amazing thing going at the Westwood Light ..."

"Yeah, I keep seeing the photos on Facebook."

Brant's face warms as he stares at her over the counter. "Those kids freaking adore her."

I smile at that, feeling a tickle of inspiration. Maybe I can write about an orphanage. Orphan kids. Maybe a sci-fi setting with orphans. A world full of orphans ...

Ugh, I've gotten desperate and messy. My inspiration is everywhere. *Quiet down in there, head. Not everything is a source of inspiration!*

Brant nudges me. "You ever heard from Riley after graduation?"

I shake my head. "Nope. Total mystery. I always figured she got lucky with mister sweater vest and married him. Maybe she moved to Wisconsin and owns a cabin with a wraparound porch. I have no idea. Tomas, however ..."

"Tomas? Oh, Sam's bassoon-suckin' dude. Yeah, what about him?"

I chortle. Brant's going to think I'm dicking with him. "Dude. You know we went back home for Thanksgiving last year—the last time we saw you guys. Well, I might've forgotten to mention that we sorta ran into Tomas. It was a total fluke, running into him. Maybe he saw on Facebook that we were in town or something. But ..." I fight laughter.

"Keep me in suspense," Brant begs me. "No, really. Just never get to your point. I'll stand here and nurse this beer for hours if I have to."

"I don't think it's bassoons that Tomas *sucks* anymore."

Brant's eyes flash. "Say what?"

"Tomas is gay," I finish.

Brant had gone for another swig. Now he's choking on that swig as he slams his bottle down and screws his wet eyes onto mine. "No way!" he finally sputters when he stops coughing. "You're totally fucking with me!"

"Babe," calls out Nell from the other room. "Watch your damned language."

Brant lifts his head. "Tomas is gay!" he calls out to her. "Tomas! Sam's ex!"

Nell blinks. "Really?"

Sam nods, then pushes a finger into the bridge of her glasses. "It's probably my fault." She eyes me across the room. "Just kidding," she deadpans. "I know you hate when I say that."

I chuckle, then nod back at Brant. "Yeah, it's no joke. Though, to be accurate and fair to Tomas's life journey, as it were, I think he identifies as asexual.

But he prefers males for ... uh, he had a word for it ... for 'companions'. He likes kissing them. He likes cuddling with them. But he, like, never engages sexually with anyone. Or so he told us over three mugs of green tea and a plate of spring rolls."

"Dude, that almost sounds like you from freshman year," says Brant.

I shove him for that, which surprisingly almost knocks him off balance as he laughs. I've noticed that Brant's put on several pounds over the years. Maybe even ten. Yet he still has retained his oddly charming, boyish face and that twinkle in his blue eyes. "I know you wanted me to be gay *so* badly," I tease him, "but if you only knew what I was up to freshman year ..."

"Oh yeah? What were you up to, mister *subversive*?"

I glance over at the beautiful woman on the couch next to Nell, the one with the stylish glasses, the cute black pixie hair (she recently cut off her long hair and donated it), the green dress with the slit up the side, and the brand new musical note tattoo running up her shoulder. "A pretty girl in my poetry class," I murmur, staring longingly at her. "That's what I was up to."

Brant gives me a skeptical look. "Forgive my doubt. But seeing you trying to get in with a pretty girl in your poetry class is a bit of a hard sell for me."

"You have it wrong. See, I didn't realize ... that *she* was the poetry all along." I smile, thinking back fondly on the day Sam smacked me over the back of my head with her notebook and asked me to be her partner. If I'd only known that someday I would be her *life* partner ... but I was young, and the beauty of my future to come was something I couldn't possibly grasp. "Best year of my life."

When Brant follows my sight to the couch, he puts two and two together and nods knowingly. "I think the best years are still to come, my man."

"That much is true," I agree, then wonder if my story should be about poetry. Are the characters in my head poets? Orphan poets? I shake my head, as if literally trying to dislodge my characters from the seats in which they're all stubbornly sulking. "You and Nell ready to go soon? We should head out now if we want to be on time. The premiere tonight is completely sold out, every single seat, from what Clayton told me, so it'll be packed and might take us time to get situated."

Brant's face tightens up, then he sets down his bottle, unfinished, and gives me an awkward nod. "Yeah, man. Let's get our booties shakin'. Zara, Nell," he calls out. "You two ready to go?"

I note Brant's sudden discomfort, but I don't say anything. Sam and Nell turn and look at us as if we're the rudest individuals on the planet for interrupting their engrossing conversation about— whatever gory, horrifying murder it is that's got their minds enslaved. I'm pretty sure I'll be introduced to it tomorrow and then binge watching all eleven or twelve seasons from now until New Year's.

After a bus ride, taking the subway, and a jolly six-block walk, we're standing in a lobby packed with excited murmurs and conversation. There are so many people here to see Dessie's show that, even though I was previously warned, I still find myself floored. I knew Dessie's career had majorly taken off over the years (she even starred in a week-long run of a show in London), but I must have lost track of exactly how large her following has become. Circles of excited high school theatre seniors are spouting off about how excited they are to get Desdemona's autograph on their programs afterwards. Students from every university in the state are here blabbering on about their own dreams, projects, and how the work of Desdemona inspired them to pursue their craft.

And to think that just a handful of years ago, little Dessie was afraid she'd never live up to the grand Lebeau name.

Oh, my characters could be theatre student orphans. Theatre student orphans who like poetry!

Ugh. I can't shut my mind off, ever.

"Sam! Sam!"

I turn to the sound of Victoria's voice as she cuts through the crowd. She clutches Sam's side the moment she's within reach and gives her a quick hug.

"Hey, Vicki," I call out to her.

Her eyes turn into that of a demon's as she slowly turns her head toward me. "My ... name ... is ... *Victoria.*"

My eyes flash. "Uh, sorry."

She turns dainty the next second. "No worries, sweetness! Brant! Nell!" she calls out as she rises to her tippy-toes and gives them a wave. "I'm so glad you all made it! I just wanted to find you guys and make sure that Operation Brell was still a go."

My face scrunches up. "Brell?"

Sam shoots me her flat-lipped smile. "Brant and Nell. Brell. It was my horrible idea."

I fight a laugh. "I accept your apology."

"I didn't apologize," she sasses me, deadpan.

Brant steps forward suddenly and leans in toward Victoria. "Are we, uh, gonna see them before the show? Clayton and Dessie? Or, uh, not until the after party? Or—?"

"After curtain call, honey," Victoria explains. "Even *I've* been banished from backstage for now, so you definitely won't be seeing them beforehand. Dessie is in her zone. Clayton's in the lighting booth going over his cues as if he hasn't been at every rehearsal and stayed late for hours every single night during tech week." She grips Brant's arm. "Trust me, it'll be a complete and total surprise when they see you after the show. I can't f ... freaking wait." She had to edit herself on account of Zara's presence, which she just now takes note of. She bends down. "Hey there, sweetie! You excited to see the show?"

Zara scowls and hides behind Brant's legs.

"Ah, sorry," mumbles Brant, then gives his daughter a little pat on her head. "This is Aunt Victoria, sweetie. She's a good friend of Aunt

Dessie."

"I'm Zara," the four-year-old states bashfully, still hiding behind Brant's legs.

"So ... the surprise. Cool," sputters Brant, swallowing hard, his eyes glassy with nerves. "Good. We'll be the ... total surprise after the show. Can't wait."

Victoria eyes him suspiciously. "You okay, Brant? You look like you're about to shit a diamond."

"I'm—nah, I'm fantastic." He laughs it off, then shrugs and thrusts his hands into his pockets. "I'm great. Cool as a tool. Or pool. Or whatever the kids say. Where are the bathrooms? That way, I see the sign. I'll be right back." He heads off, vanishing into a thicket of twenty-somethings from NYU.

Nell's hand is clung to little Zara's tightly the next second, as little Zara apparently needs a new place to hide. Nell shrugs at the rest of us. "It's ... been a long time since Brant's seen either of them. He's nervous because we had to turn down the last several times they invited us on account of us being entirely unable to stop being so goddamned fertile."

"Bless you, child," murmurs Victoria.

Nell shrugs. "We're going to have to put up

with him being weird for a bit, I think."

Victoria nods. "Figured that's what was going on. Oh, where's Eric?" she asks suddenly, turning toward me. "Wasn't he coming with you guys?"

I shake my head. "He's going to have to see the show tomorrow or the next day. Bailey's got him by the nuts, last I heard, and they're being forced to do some sort of other obligation. Shitty, I know, but Bailey's turned into a bossy little queen, so ..."

Sam's hand runs up my back, then comes to rest on my shoulder, pulling me against her side. "It's too bad he can't be here with us. I do ... *love* ... that Bailey kid."

I shoot Sam a teasing look. "You just like reminding Bailey that the day you met him, you nearly karate-chopped him in half and made him soil his big boy underwear."

Sam shrugs innocently, then slides her hand up to the back of my head, as if to nurse an old, old wound. "I seem to have a knack for catching boys by surprise the first time they meet me."

At that, I grin, then bring my lips to Sam's for a deep, breath-stealing kiss.

"Eww!" shouts Zara.

Sam and I pull apart with laughter while Nell

quietly admonishes her daughter. "That's not nice! Do you remember what daddy told you before we left home?"

Zara scowls. "Yes. Cake. *Sowwy.*"

"Good. Do it for the cake, sweetheart." Nell gives her daughter a kiss on the top of the head, then smiles at the rest of us.

I smile back. "Oh, if only little Zara knew how you and *daddy* met, she'd be 'eww'-ing until the New Year's Eve ball drops in Times Square."

"Don't encourage her," Nell warns me, pursing her lips.

The lights in the lobby dim twice, signaling that the show is about to start. Victoria chirps, her hands practically trembling as she scurries off. Two minutes later, Brant has returned, and then the five of us head into the auditorium to find our seats, which are surprisingly close to the stage—aisle seats in the second row, at that. Brant fidgets so much that his chair won't stop squeaking. Nell preens her daughter's dark hair.

Sam is flipping through the program, reading the bios. She looks up at me and catches me staring at her. "What?" she blurts. "Is there something on my face?"

"Yeah, a kiss." I press my lips to her cheek. "Oh, look. Another." I go for her other cheek. "And yet another." I peck at her nose.

I finally get a giggle out of Sam as she pushes my face away from hers. "You're especially playful tonight. Almost made me forget it's Christmas in a couple weeks. It totally doesn't feel like December, what with our busy past few months and your blog column and ..." She reels, thinking of all the craziness and deadlines and work our life has been filled with lately.

I smile evilly. "Just wait for the snow, sweetheart."

"Ugh." Sam faces forward, staring at the stage despondently. "I hate snow."

I wrap my arms around her and hug her side, then draw my lips to her ear where I put another kiss. She flinches, smiling and tickled by the sensitive place where I put my mouth. "*Is it bad,*" I whisper, "*that even though Brant and Nell just arrived, I already can't wait for them to leave so that I can have my way with you in our apartment?*"

Sam's face flushes from chin to forehead. "*It was* your *idea to have them stay with us instead of getting a hotel room,*" she reminds me in as much of a hushed whisper.

"Bad, bad idea."

"We'll punish you later for it."

"How?"

"I'll let you pick something out of our box of 'toys' to use on you."

"I can't wait."

The lights fade out, and soon, the audience is brought to complete silence as the stage swells with a rich blue light. The artful attention and detail of color, shape, and intensity is all Clayton's genius at work right before our eyes as we drink in the visuals. Then Dessie walks on stage from a simple door, and more light pools about her, bringing her to life like an angel.

Ooh. Angels who are student poets—*and* orphans.

Shut up, brain.

Soon, Dessie's story overpowers any thought I could possibly give to the nonexistent one in my own head. It's a simple concept, but moves my soul to a place of inspired excitement as I watch the story unfold. It's about a relationship counselor with a screw loose named Emily—played by Dessie, who named the character after the first role she was cast in at Klangburg University—and she sings a song about how she can pull any two people together, keep them happy for life, but can't seem to do a damned thing for herself. Her office secretary—a cute and totally gay sidekick—suffers a similar fate of being perpetually single, despite going on a date with a new guy every single weekend of his life. "*I'm a serial datist,*" he sings in his own song.

Then Dessie's character Emily is faced with her most troubling clients yet: a sassy woman dressed head to toe in rich black and red (Victoria's genius shining through) and a lively man dressed head to toe in vivid creams and whites. They are a married couple who are constantly at war with one another and desperately need Emily's help.

But they are not who they seem. As it turns out, the woman is actually Death herself, and the man is Life. "*We have tried everything to save our marriage,*" sings Death in her hilariously grim, powerhouse voice that rings with the dark entitlement of a diva. "*Our careers get in the way!*"

"*My wife is afraid of an overpopulated world!*" sings Life in a loose, jazzy voice that complements Death in its slinkiness and swagger. "*What's wrong with more Life, Death?*"

"*What's wrong with more Death, Life?*" she sings right back, sassy as ever. The line earns a punch of laughter from the audience. Maybe it's the way she pops her hips on the high note. "*My career only exists because of yours!*"

"*My sweet love,*" Life sings right back. "*Our work complements one another, don't you see? You complete me.*"

The line is funny and ironic and all that—and the audience goes wild—but I find myself pulled in by that line more than I'm likely expected to. I even lose the next part of Life and Death's playful banter as I get lost in my thoughts, yet again, and grow curious about why the characters in my head keep so silent.

What has gotten me so ... blocked up?

Then I turn to Sam, whose full attention is attached to the stage like a sleeve to a shirt, every stitch of her excitement sewn tightly to every ringing note. Surely Sam is appreciating every piece of music in this show; it always fascinates her, learning the way that others tell stories using song and clever lyrics. She's gotten so much braver at stringing pretty words together and setting them to her music. She was positively terrified the first time

we sat at a piano years ago and worked through some lyric-writing exercises. I had only half an idea of what I was doing (and maybe so did she), but together, we made a pretty kick-ass team.

A burst of music brings my attention back to the stage where we discover the real reason for Life and Death's arrival into Emily's office: They had scheduled an appointment there today because Emily—loyal relationship counselor—was next on Death's list. At the encouragement of Life, Death decides to strike a deal with the counselor: If she is able to save Life and Death's marriage in no more than three appointments, Death shall overlook Emily's name on her list and allow her to live.

Matters grow quite urgent suddenly for poor counselor Emily by the act break, and the fate of her life hangs in the balance of whether she's able to save the relationship between Life and Death itself.

Nell and Brant and their child rush to the bathroom when the stage goes dark, the curtains draw, and the auditorium lights come back up. Sam turns to me. "That was an interesting first act. Not like I expected at all."

I find myself thinking about that first semester of college, which feels like a lifetime ago. I picture her face—before her grand Dessie-inspired makeover sophomore year—and feel a surge of passion burst through me. "An unusual first act," I agree.

"But I liked it." Her brows pull together. "What are you looking at me like that for?"

I lift an eyebrow. "Sorry?"

"You have this look in your eye like you've seen a poltergeist with thirteen boobs and a penis on its forehead."

I let out a bark of laughter and shake my head. "The hell do you come up with this stuff, Sam?"

She shrugs, then smiles her flat-lipped smile. "Funny you should ask, considering the strange and beautiful things that come out of your head, mister masturbation monster."

I gape with mock offense. "How dare you!"

"Do you think we should get married?"

The question softens my humorous pearl-clutching gape to a genuine look of bewilderment. "I ... W-Wait. What?"

"I'm not proposing to you," she explains dryly. "You know me better than that."

I blink. "Why did you ask that, then? About getting married?"

"Brant and Nell finally tied the knot a few years

back. Dessie and Clayton are together. Even Life and Death are married, apparently. Eric is pretty much one step away from Bailey clicking the immortal chains around his ankle, if we're being honest here."

I nod. "True. Very true. But—"

"And I know we've sorta defined ourselves as the ... *unconventional relationship type*. My mom and dad are ... somewhere between husband-and-wife and traveling swingers, if I let my imagination go to certain places."

"Kudos to them."

"Your sister Devin is a bit of a man-eater, from what you've told me, and might not settle down until she's sixty, if ever. Poor thing."

"Poor thing," I agree.

"But maybe she's happy being the way she is. Why do we presume that if someone isn't married or coupled up ... that they aren't happy? Some people are *more* lonely in relationships."

My eyes flash. "Sam. Are we breaking up?"

She smirks, which is nearly undetectable with her dry demeanor; her smirks come in the form of a twitch at the right corner of her sexy lips. "No. Just the opposite. I don't want to be with anyone else. But I've always felt like marriage is this ... archaic declaration of possession of another human being. Love should never be owned."

I shrug. "Well, it could also be seen as a commitment to the one you love. I don't think all marriage is a bad thing, really."

"So you *do* want to get married?"

I scowl at her. Is she trying to trap me into an answer, or coax a truth out of me that I'm totally not intentionally withholding from her? "I want to be with you. You're the only one I want."

"Me too. I mean, *you*. You're the only one I want."

"Whether you want to marry or not, that's up to you. Or ... us. We decided we're okay being us without a paper to prove it. I think it was also sorta our way to defy the heterosexist normative. Or whatever we called it years ago."

"The baleful beast of white picket fences and screaming children, I believe was the phrase."

"We can just be us," I tell her, bringing a hand up to her hair, feeling the prickles of her short hair at the back of her head and the soft, longer strands that trickle down. "The way we are. Sam and D. All that matters is that I love you ... and you love me."

"That's a Barney song."

"I almost sang the words," I admit.

Sam leans over the armrest and kisses me. I close my eyes and melt into her kiss, feeling a warmth spread through my body. Any of my limbs that were made numb throughout the first act—when the lukewarm air in this building has done little to nothing to fight off the sweeping cold front outside—are on fire in an instant.

Somewhere between the fire of her kiss, and the poetry of theatre student orphans in my head, and the promise of snow outside, I hear the first whispers of characters in my head. It's the first whispers in months.

My eyes flash open.

Sam pulls away, startled. "What is it?"

"The characters ... They're *speaking*."

Sam gapes, then hugs me tightly. She knows exactly what I mean. Then, in my ear, she murmurs, "And the musicians are playing in mine. And not a single one of them plays the bassoon."

To that, I laugh, then plant a kiss right on her lips. All the characters in my head, a second ago sulking, leap from their chairs and cheer. *Even my creative insanity is, for the first time in a long time, happy.*

Nell

Okay, I won't lie. I was expecting this play to suck. Like, majorly suck.

Like, the second we learn that the married couple is actually Life and Death, I rolled my eyes so hard that I figuratively had to chase them halfway down the aisle to get them back.

I don't know why Desdemona and I never quite clicked. Even after reconciling, even after seeing how good of a person she is and how deeply her heart runs for her friends ... I still can't shake the feeling that I've never truly been welcome in her circle. I'm the outsider. Everyone else is loveable, or cool, or sexy, or interesting.

I'm just a black hole of despair.

It's probably the dark demons inside me that will keep me pessimistic for the rest of my days. Fight them as I might, I'm doomed to see the worst in others ... and the world in general.

But despite all of that, Dessie's show surprised me in the end. Yes, I got a touch emotional. Me, Nell, Queen of Darkness ... was moved. When the curtains fall at the conclusion of the show, I caught myself applauding with more vigor than I anticipated. Maybe it was the biting humor of Death's ceaseless bitchiness that spoke volumes to me, as if she was me. Or perhaps it was the carefree jovialness of Life that so reminded me of Brant trying to cheer me up whenever I'm in one of my self-hating can't-make-a-single-piece-of-art moods.

Maybe there's more depth to Dessie than I ever gave her credit for.

And maybe none of that matters at all, since I'll never truly have a place among her elite posse.

"You look especially happy," notes Brant when I reunite with him in the lobby after taking Zara to the restroom. "Was it the ending?"

I have no idea where he's seeing the happiness in my expression, but I smile at him anyway and let our daughter run up and wrap her arms around his legs. "Have you reconnected with your childhood boyfriend and his super talented wife yet?"

Brant narrows his eyes. "Was the play really that bad for you?"

For some reason, I can't exactly let out how much it moved me. I always deflect my emotions and act like I'm too cool for school. It's a quality of mine that even I can't stand. "It was alright," I tell him with a lilt to my voice that suggests I might have genuinely enjoyed it.

Brant, being my husband and all, truly "hears" me between the lines. "Wow. It really spoke to you that much, huh? Was it Death? She was *totally* written after you, I just know it." Brant smiles knowingly—or perhaps tauntingly. "I knew you had a weak spot for Dessie. I think you like her."

I frown. "Don't even with that."

He chuckles and looks off through the crowd. His face tightens at once when he sees them. "Shit."

I smirk and put an arm around my man. "You know, they still don't know we're here. We *could* sneak off and not let them know that we left our twins with your parents, paid for plane tickets, flew all the way out here to support them, and—"

"Okay, okay, I get your point well enough without the sarcasm," he murmurs to me with a humored smirk.

"Who am I without my sarcasm?"

Brant puts a nervous peck on my cheek, his full

attention clearly on the two individuals across the crowded lobby. He looks me in the eye. "I can do this, right?"

A smile finally breaks across my own stubborn face. "You're so cute when you're nervous."

He wrinkles his face. "I'm not nervous! I'm perfectly—"

"Daddy," Zara sings up to him, still clinging to his legs. "You're *neeervous.*"

Brant glances between the both of us. "You two need to find yourself some more faith in Daddy! Hey." He picks Zara right up, settling her in his arms and bringing her eyes level with his. "Aren't you excited to see your Uncle Clayton and Aunt Dessie? You haven't seen them in person in a very, very long time."

"I see them all the time!" Zara argues back.

"Their faces on a tiny metal device doesn't count, you goof."

I notice a slight shift in the crowd, reminding me oddly of the way branches sway when disturbed by an unexpected wind. Then I see them—both of them—being ushered our way. "Um, Brant ..."

"Yeah, babe?"

"Not to freak you out, but I think Sam is

bringing *them* to *us*."

Brant's eyes turn to glass and he freezes, his stare locked on mine. He was clearly counting on a few more minutes—maybe even half an hour, at the slow rate in which this lobby is clearing—to steel himself before facing the Clay and the Dess. But now that particular luxury is stolen from him in one swift instant, and he has exactly ten seconds before he's confronted with the very thing he's feared since we first stepped foot on that shaky, turbulence-ridden plane so many hours ago.

Scratch that. Two seconds.

The sea of people part at once, and suddenly Sam, Dessie, and Clayton stand in front of my startled husband, who still carries Zara on his hip. For a solid handful of seconds, Brant just stares at the pair of them as if unsure whether he can remember their names. He is paralyzed.

I roll my eyes. *He's helpless.* I take a quick step forward to save him. "Great show," I tell the pair of them. "Really. I enjoyed it a lot."

Dessie's eyes flash with joy. "Nell! Brant and Nell! How did you two—?!"

"It was Sam's idea," I blurt out. "We left our twins with Brant's mom and dad. They're in their terrible twos, so basically ... they aren't very travel-friendly. We pawned off the demon spawn."

Dessie blinks, unsure what to make of all of that.

"In other words, we're horrible parents," Brant summarizes, breaking the ice.

That makes Dessie laugh finally, then she shakes her head and gives Brant a half-hug. "That's the last thing you two are. Hey you, Queen Zara!" she sings, bringing her face to our daughter's and putting a kiss on her forehead. "How are you? Still ruling the Underworld? I heard you got a solo in your school choir!"

"It's more like a preschool scream-along than it is a choir," Brent leans into Dessie to amend, "but thanks for the kind words."

Dessie laughs again. *She's just full of laughs and giggles tonight, isn't she?* "Zara, you are so big! Soon, you're going to be as tall as your beautiful mother!"

The compliment rolls over my head and hops down my back and is gone as quickly as it came. I step forward and pull Zara from Brant's hip to give him space to acknowledge Clayton—as well as the use of his hands, in case he wants to utilize any of that new sign language he's been practicing.

As soon as he has his hands free, however, he seems to not know what to do with them. He stares at Clayton with his mouth open—saying nothing—and his hands are hovering somewhere near his hips.

I wonder if I just took away his shield.

Then, finally, at long last, Clayton makes the first move, and it isn't in the form of words. He takes one step forward—considering his muscular size and stride, it only takes a single step—and then he wraps his arms around his buddy and pulls him in, squeezing a grunt of surprise out of him.

Dessie and I watch, likely with completely different thoughts going on in our heads. Dessie appears to be full of the kind of wistful delight that expresses itself in misty eyes, clasped hands, and a swelling heart.

And I'm just waiting for Brant to shit his pants already.

The boys finally separate, and then Clayton says something too quiet for me to hear.

Apparently it's too quiet for anyone else to hear either. "Sorry?" Brant mutters, using his mouth instead of his hands, despite how much we practiced.

Clayton speaks up, his soft voice miraculously tripling in its volume. "I'm really glad you came."

Relief and joy settles on Brant's face. He's such a dummy, having worried this whole time. "Me too. Eden and Dalia send their love. I think. I'm pretty sure they do. My parents have them. I'm just … I'm sure they'll be fine, yeah. Um. And I … I wanted to see your show. Dessie's show," he amends with a sweep of his hand toward her, almost accidentally knocking his daughter in the face. "And your … your genius lighting. It was really … really …"

While Brant searches for the word, I find myself marveling once again at how incredible Clayton's skill at reading lips must be. Or maybe it's a deaf thing. Or a Brant-and-Clayton thing. But Clayton seems to follow his every word with ease.

Still unable to find the word, Brant changes his tack, finally opting for a sign. Or perhaps it was what he was searching for all along. He brings a hand to his chin, then tosses it outward.

Clayton quirks an eyebrow. "It was really 'thank you'?"

Brant shakes his head. "No, sorry. Ugh. Shit. I meant … It was really …" And then he does the same damned sign again.

I roll my eyes. We practiced these signs a hundred times. Literally. *It's his nerves. He's a mess.*

Then, out of nowhere, Zara stamps her little feet right up to Clayton and shouts, "It was really *good!*" at Clayton, then brings a hand to her chin and pulls it down to slap the palm of her other hand—*Good.*

If I thought the look of surprise on Clayton's face from seeing his best friend after so many years was uncharacteristically expressive, it holds nothing to the look on his face now. He crouches down to Zara's height, excited, and gives her one of his rare, lopsided smiles. "You can speak with your hands!" he exclaims, slurring slightly on the word "hands", his eyes lit up. "Impressive!"

She giggles, then makes two thumbs-up and rotates them awkwardly in the air. Then she makes the sign—*Good*—again. Then she does something else I can't quite figure out.

Clayton chuckles, then starts making slow and deliberate signs right back to her, after which she giggles.

Brant and I share a look. *They're communicating and we have no idea what they're saying.*

Dessie, however, smiles knowingly and leans

into me. "Your daughter is the most adorable thing in the world. She's telling Clayton she thought the show was good, she liked the clothing—*costumes, I'm guessing she means*—and that she fell asleep. Also, she had fun. Fun, fun, fun. *She likes that sign.* And she's very cold. Oh, and she just said she wants cake. She earned it." Dessie's face wrinkles up, and she glances at Brant. "Apparently *Daddy* said she earned it ...?"

Brant turns to us, bewildered. "It was bribery. I'm a bad daddy."

"Cake bribery," mumbles Dessie with mock disapproval.

"Also, I know she's been learning signs," Brant goes on, "but I had no idea she learned the sign for *cake*. We're doomed."

Dessie finds that to be the most hilarious thing in the world, emitting a musical symphony of laughs in every harmonious note possible. "Of *course* she learned that sign! Children learn the signs they desperately need to communicate. And this little one *needs* cake."

Zara spins around and faces Dessie, her eyes wide. "Can I have a piece??"

"Of course! But you have to be a patient girl. There will be *aaaaall* the cake you can imagine at my after party." Dessie's face freezes for a second as she glances between Brant and I. "Um ... she's allowed to come to the after party, right? I can't guarantee how appropriate or kid-friendly it will be. I didn't know y'all were coming."

"Y'all." Brant grins. "Listen to her. A New Yorker speaking like a true Texan, even though she only spent four tiny years there."

I run a hand along Zara's back, toying with her soft hair. "She'll be fine. Between Brant's Xbox and my art, the girls have sadly been subjected to about every possible thing a human being can, and neither one has even turned five yet."

Zara turns around. "So I can have cake?? Have I been good enough?"

"Yes, you have. And yes, of course you can have cake." I kiss the top of Zara's head.

Dessie looks like she's about to explode with emotion like confetti from a piñata. Again, this might be my own darkness determinedly trying to push forward to make a tragedy out of everything, but I can't help entertaining the notion that Dessie is just riding the high of her opening night, and she would be clapping her hands and near tears about anything in the world at all, regardless of Brant and

my presence here. We just happen to be here like any other audience member. If it was another day, she'd probably express just as much excitement in seeing us as she would if her Monday morning barista accidentally put an extra shot of espresso in her coffee.

We aren't special. We aren't a part of their lives anymore.

And I think I sorta never was, no matter how hard I tried to be "the girl people like". I'll never be that girl.

"I'm so glad you two are here!" Dessie exclaims, as if she was aware of and is directly challenging the shadowy realm that is my emotional landscape.

And just as forced, just as put-on, I stretch my lips into a smile and say, "We are, too."

I genuinely hope my emotions match my words soon. On some level, I really do mean it.

A while later, Zara, Brant, and I are at the enormous (even for Texan standards) townhome of Dessie's parents where the after party is being hosted. Or maybe it's their second or third home, I can't be sure. Brant explained it on the cab ride over, but I was too distracted staring out the window and wondering why I can't just be happy like everyone else is. Brant is getting to see his best friend. Dessie is enjoying the exhilaration sparking between them. Zara is about to stay up way past her bedtime with a bellyful of triple chocolate cake.

And I'm busy wearing a smile, begging for everyone to not dread my presence when they look my way, and trying to convince myself that the world isn't bleak and horrible and lonely.

The one and only thing that makes me feel happy is Brant and the family we've created. My Zara. My goblin princess Eden and my black-bat-loving Dalia. I can turn around and go right back home, and all the joy of a happily-ever-after will rush right back into me like the comfort of a warm blanket and hot chocolate on a cold winter night.

They're all I need. Not Dessie's approval. Not Clayton's approval.

Just my family.

Zara and Brant are at the long, extravagant dessert table where my little girl is getting her long-awaited piece of cake ... after impatiently waiting in a long line of others serving themselves first. I'm standing by a tall glass window overlooking the street with Sam at my side as she tells me about a composition she's writing that's confounding her.

The noise in the room is quite loud, as if we're right back in the lobby of that theater, except now we're surrounded by people who are making me feel more and more underdressed and unworthy by the second.

"I mean, it's not that I think I *need* a reed pipe in my composition, but ... I'm just lacking the right voice, the right *punch* of ... obnoxiousness. And I think—"

"What about an oboe?" I suggest, drawing from what limited musical knowhow I have swimming around in my brain.

"Yes, right. Very good. Except ..." Sam bites her lip and pushes a finger at her glasses. "Except I don't think it's enough of a ... a ... Ugh, maybe I just ... just need to ..."

"Not everything you create is going to be clean and perfect. Sometimes you gotta dirty it up, don't you think?" I catch myself in half a chuckle as I nod toward Dmitri across the room, who's signing back and forth with Clayton. "Don't fall into Dmitri's trap of letting a story torture him for months before he finally realizes his plot can't work out perfectly in the end. Some characters gotta die. Or move away. Or have some horrible, inescapable flaw that the reader may, in fact, never fall in love with. It just happens. Some characters ... aren't really meant to be loved." I fold my arms and tilt my head, my eyes finding Dessie on the other side of the room. "Some characters just get all the attention, all the love, all the favor. And some of us—"

"Are we still talking about music?"

I shut myself up and cast my gaze to the floor. *The wood flooring is so shiny in this place, I can see my reflection.* "My point is, art is messy. Don't stay in the lines so much. Draw from the things you hate. Draw from the things that make you uncomfortable. It's only from those places that something real can emerge."

"You're so fucking cool."

I lift my gaze back to Sam and blink, startled. "Huh?"

"You. Your whole ... *thing*. Back at Klangburg, I kinda thought Chloe was the one I'd connect with the most, seeing as she was the emo, black-eyeliner, punk hair type. Sorry for saying that, since I know she's one of Brant's exes and all. But the more I've gotten to know you over the years, I realize that ... of all Dessie's friends ... maybe even including Dessie herself ... I think I relate to you the most."

Daryl Banner

My eyebrows go up all on their own. I'm genuinely rendered speechless by her words.

"You have an unapologetic way of artistically expressing yourself," Sam goes on. "I admire that. I can see in your eyes that you fear things too, and you are sensitive, and ... well, maybe you're also a little intimidating."

"Intimidating?"

"And maybe when people are talking to you, they're always afraid of offending you, or of pissing you off, or of saying the wrong thing. I think it's because there's something about you that makes people want to ... impress you. You're a person of very high standards, whether you know it or not." Sam pokes at her glasses again, then bites her lip and peers into my eyes. "Is that okay to say?"

I swallow once, then give a stiff shrug, her words still unraveling me by the syllable. "Uh, sure."

"It's a good thing." She offers me a meek smile. "I ... want to be as brave and as free as you are."

"You're a New Yorker," I point out to her. "That already proves you are."

Sam chuckles at that—which is about the saddest, dullest, most adorably dry chuckle I've ever heard. "I appreciate it. But I mean artistically brave.

Artistically free."

"Just dare to be dirty. Dare to be messy."

"Messy." Sam lifts the tiny plate of cake in her hand, then pokes a finger into the vanilla cream of a pastry and dabs her own nose with it. She turns her wide eyes to me, a blob of the off-white cream hanging on her nose. "Messy?"

I fight off a laugh. Yeah, me, laughing. "Perfect."

The next moment, Sam puts her arms around me—still awkwardly carrying her plate—and holds onto me. I think this is supposed to be a hug. I'm almost fairly sure that's what this is.

I tentatively put an arm around her back, accepting it.

It's weird. Being hugged. Spontaneously. Without any apparent reason.

Something inside me softens, dying before the swelling shadows of my inner self-hate. A light is cutting through all of that—a light that's taking the form of a dab of vanilla cream at the end of Sam's nose, which is dangerously close to wiping itself on my chest.

Oddly, I don't care. I like it, in fact. I like it so much, my lips are doing a weird sort of twisty thing that feels so alien.

I think it's a smile.

An actual one.

"I miss you, Penelope," Sam tells me, half-muffled against my side.

Even Brant doesn't use my real name. But the strange intimacy that hearing my name inspires in me pulls me right out of the darkness like a drowning child from a lake. I feel the little girl in me suck in her first breath of air in years.

Then across the way, as if choreographed, I spot Dessie watching us. The look in her eye is full of happiness, watching the pair of us awkwardly hug. Dessie's eyes meet mine from across the enormous room, and then she winks at me.

"Dare to be messy," I murmur—my own odd advice—then poke my own finger into the cream on Sam's clumsily-held plate and dab my own nose. Then I half-hug Sam tighter, feeling more like a part of the "inner circle" than I've ever felt before.

Sam

It's good to be weird.

Those are the words I've embraced over the years, and they've helped me come to terms with so many aspects of my life that someday long ago tortured me.

Now, I love my mom and dad. I love that they're fantastically strange and unconventional, touring the country and living a reckless life that never sits still. I love that I have a boyfriend—life partner, companion, whatever you want to call it—who is also bisexual. I love that we can check out other guys together and laugh about it. I love that we create things together—music and words and story, all uniting in a beautiful collaboration that fulfills both our souls.

And none of it is made of the stuff you see in romantic comedies, or mainstream love stories, or on family TV.

And it's good to be weird. Because I'm happy.

Still with a gob of cream on our noses, Nell and I turn to face Dessie, who's approached us with a glass of champagne in her hand and a delighted, red-cheeked smile. "I love you two. Have I said that yet, today? You're two of my favorite people."

Nell's smile that she returns is warm, which sits strangely on her face, like an unfamiliar face at the dinner table, a guest from a faraway land. "I think your character of Death might be my spirit animal," Nell confesses.

"Oh? Samantha Hart here isn't?" teases Dessie, then nods at both of us. "Is this a new fashion trend? Rudolph the Cream-Nosed Reindeer?"

Nell winces. "My mind goes elsewhere when you word it like that."

I cough on a chuckle of my own. "Rudolph's been to a few seedy gay clubs, sounds like."

Dessie gasps. "You two are so dirty! Get your minds out of the gutter!" Then she breaks into a fit of laughter—likely facilitated by her glass of champagne, which I suspect isn't her first by far. "I just love you two even more."

"It's good to be weird," I state.

Dessie winks at me. "Indeed, it is." Then she turns to Nell. "I wanted to approach you at another time, but I suppose now is as good as any. Clayton and I might be opening a theater in the next year or so, and ... well, this may come much farther down the line ... but we want a prominent piece of art in our lobby. It's part of our whole theme and design. I was wondering if ... *you* might like to be our first featured artist."

Nell looks genuinely stunned to wordlessness. I've never seen this particular look on her face. It's almost as alien to her as the genuine smile a moment ago.

Dessie goes on. "You can think about it. You don't have to give me an answer now. Just mull it over."

"I didn't know you're opening up a theater," I blurt with my mouth full, since I just took a big fat bite of the pastry on my plate.

Dessie nods excitedly. "We haven't really told many people other than the three or four colleagues we're collaborating with to make it happen. We want to feature original works, local playwrights, artists, musicians ... We even want to host a sort of afterschool acting and writing workshop."

"I love the idea," blurts Nell. "That sounds so great. And the kids ... you'll put art into their lives."

"Well, it's not the genius of inspiring orphans by melting crayons over glass bottles, but I suppose it's a start," replies Dessie with a wink and a smile at Nell, who appears touched by the words. "Yes, I still have that photo framed at my house. You and all the kids at Westwood Light that Brant took. It's beautiful, Nell. Inspires me every day."

Nell's eyes mist over.

Okay, seriously, what's up with Nell?

After lifting her chin and apparently determined not to show any more emotion than she just did, Nell says, "Thank you," like a businessman, then lets out a little smile and adds, "That means a lot to me."

"Like I said, you two are two of my favorites in the whole world." Dessie glances over her shoulder. "I better go check the door. I think Eric might be here sans Bailey. They had drama. What else is new?" She rolls her eyes. "I'm going to go give him shit for not making my opening." Dessie throws us another wink, then saunters off.

I glance up at Nell, who is still visibly fighting off tears, if I'm interpreting what I'm seeing correctly. "Are you alright?" I ask. "Is it the baby?"

"I'm barely two months pregnant," she mutters.

"I'm fine. I'm happy, really." Then she smiles, a tiny twinkle in her eye. "Happier than I've been in a long time."

Her words make me smile despite myself. I pop the rest of the pastry in my mouth, then state, "We should probably wipe our noses clean before our boys see us. They're going to think it's a competition and plant their faces into the vanilla cream pies."

"You're right," Nell agrees, then we take our napkins and wipe off one another's noses like a pair of chimpanzees picking bugs out of one another's hair.

Yeah, weird and slightly gross analogy, but I don't care. That's just me, isn't it?

And it's good to be weird.

The party is crashed a moment later by an army of students from the local colleges who supported Dessie over the years and are somehow associated with a high-school-helping program Mr. Lebeau runs—I don't really know the details, to be honest. But I do know they all worship Dessie, including the very shiny ground upon which she strolls.

Amidst the mess of new arrivals, my pathway toward Dmitri is quickly blocked, and I soon find myself swimming through a crowd like a lost damsel in a forest of misty mystery. Which is pretty much an adequate way to describe the music that's trying to happen in my head and at my piano at home. Nell wanted me to play something for Zara before we left, but then it was time to go. To be frank, I'm not sure I would've had anything in me. Nothing new, at least.

Dmitri and I both have been in a rut. It seems like he just catapulted his way out, and all it took was seeing Dessie's show tonight to ignite that spark in him again. I'm happy for him, seeing as he can be utterly moody and awful when the characters aren't speaking.

But the music hasn't been silent in a long time. Now, I've gotten so desperate that I'm picturing reed instruments in my latest composition.

Reed instruments.

You know. Like a bassoon.

Lord help me.

It's not Tomas's fault that he enjoyed playing bassoons so much. It's not his fault that I'm forever cursed to gather bile in the back of my throat and spots in my eyes whenever I hear the totally unsexy hum of that horrid woodwind.

My talk with Nell was a good one, but I'm not sure if I can be like her and ... *dare to be messy*. My music is all about control. Measures. Precise notes. Harmonies. A delicate balance of tempo and focus and intensity. It's why Dmitri and I create so well; we're both so damned anal retentive, creatively speaking. I keep spreadsheets on my unfinished projects, for Pete's sake.

Cream on my nose is one thing. *How am I supposed to be messy with my music?*

"Dear God," comes a voice from my side, "where in fuck's hell's butthole do they keep the wine?"

My eyes go wide and I turn. "Eric?"

He jumps, then slaps a hand to his chest. "Samantha Hart. My arch nemesis! Just kidding, me loves you." He throws an arm around me for a lazy hug. I smell the reek of alcohol on his breath. "Are you doing well, honey? Where's Dessie?"

Also maybe marijuana. I can't tell. He smells very herby. "She's being assaulted by the theatrical student body of New York."

"Sounds like the name of a porn I watched." He brings a glass of champagne I didn't notice he had to his lips, takes a plentiful gulp, then faces me with his glassy eyes squinted. "Where's Dmitri?"

I point. "Somewhere that way."

"Hmm."

I study Eric for a moment. I've drawn my own conclusions, but don't want to step on his toes or be presumptuous. Despite how cool-mannered and polite he was back in college, he's grown into a pretty touchy individual. (Dessie tried to lovingly talk to him about it once, but he bit her head off and then expounded—at length—about how he doesn't need a lecture on how to be a decent human being, and to save her lectures for Bailey when he's off his meds.) So, knowing how sensitive he can get, I simply play dumb and ask, "How has your night been?"

Eric answers with a roll of his eyes, then he freezes, as if suddenly unable to keep up his don't-give-a-poop-about-anything attitude. Then, his face collapses with his shoulders and he shakes his head. "Bailey is too much. Bailey is too much, and I don't know if I can do it anymore."

Oh, shit. This is more than I bargained for.

"You wanna ... sit somewhere and talk?" I offer.

Eric eyes me, furrowing his brow. "You? Dead-eyed Sam? *You* want to talk to me about my failing relationship?"

I blink. "Or we can just stuff our faces at the dessert table."

He puts a hand to his belly. "I really shouldn't. I gotta watch my figure."

"There's triple chocolate cake."

"Let's do it."

The pair of us cut through the room, which is approximately twenty-six times easier with a powerhouse like Eric ungraciously shoving people out of the way (I apologized to each one), and before long, we're at the table with plates of cake, chocolate-dipped strawberries, and cheese.

Eric really, really wanted his cheese.

"So I don't think that Bailey understands the concept of *boundaries*," Eric is in the middle of explaining, "and I'd love to give him a lesson, but really, how many times do I have to explain to him that accompanying me to every single one of my rehearsals is ... well ... clingy? Ooh, he *hates* that word. Clingy. Even when I describe a *sweater* as clingy, his eyes burn red."

I promise I'm paying attention to Eric. It's just that the cake turned out to be a thousand times tastier than I previously counted on, and I'm genuinely stuffing my face, and I have no idea what the first half of our conversation was about. "He sounds clingy," I mutter through my mouthful, crumbs dancing like snowflakes from my lips.

"And yeah, sure, maybe it's because he loves me. But when someone is like that, isn't it also a strong indicator that ... oh, I don't know ... maybe he doesn't *trust* me? I've never cheated on him. I never even *looked* at another guy. But then when I told him about Dmitri and I—" He cuts himself off and stares down at me. He's about a head taller than I am. "I don't mean to dig up bad blood, if that's weird to you that ... that Dmitri and I, like ..."

"Nope. Doesn't bother me a bit."

"Really?"

"Not at all. It's kinda hot, actually." I bite the end of a chocolate-dipped strawberry. It literally bursts to life in my mouth with flavor.

"Ugh. Maybe we should date, you and I. If Dmitri will let me. I wish Bailey was more like you. Hey, can you scare the shit out of him again like you did the day y'all first met? He mentions that story to me every time I bring you up in conversation. He *adores* you."

I smile. "Maybe you need a couples counselor. Like Life and Death did in Dessie's show."

"You know, I don't know why she's making a fuss about me missing her opening night. I came to both of the invite-only preview performances earlier this week." Eric shrugs, staggers slightly, then downs the rest of his champagne before discarding the glass right in the middle of the dessert table—totally not where it ought to go. "Nell and Brant have had their bumpy moments, especially with all their kids and whatnot. Maybe they'll have advice for me."

I glance across the room, but can't see Nell through all the fancily-dressed people. "I think the play hit a personal note for her. Especially since she related so much to Death."

"Ooh, right. In act two, when you find out—"

"—that Death is pregnant with Life's baby. Yeah. Then the counselor Emily points it out, saying that *life* is growing inside Death, that if that isn't an indication that their relationship is 'doomed' to work out, she doesn't know what is."

"Then Death touches her and kills her."

"Yeah." I lick a stray bit of chocolate off my lip.

Eric smiles suddenly. "But then Life brings her back after Death is gone, and Emily gets a second chance at everything." He turns melancholy for a second, his shoulders slouched. "I wish I could get a second chance at everything. I'd do it so differently, Sam. Everything. So, so different."

I take his plate, put both his and mine down, then take his hands into mine. Eric lifts his eyebrows, confused, as I turn to face him importantly. "Life gets messy, Eric. Things aren't meant to work out cleanly. People get hurt. People make mistakes. People hang on to regrets the rest of their lives, but they also hang on to hopes and dreams. Just dare to be messy. Don't worry about living the perfect life. In fact, you ought to embrace its imperfectness. Embrace how stupid you were, and how stupid you can be, and how stupid you'll probably still be ten more years from now. And have fun with it, and throw a party in honor of the fact that we're all here, we're all making mistakes, and we're all stupid."

Eric presses his lips together for a moment before speaking. "So what you're telling me is ... I'm stupid."

"And I'm stupid, too," I go on. "I'm stupid for denying myself the beauty ..." *I can't believe I'm about to say this.* "... the beauty of the bassoon for so long. We need to get messy, Eric, and stop defining our life by only the things that go right and cleanly and perfectly."

Eric tilts his head, studying me. "A perfect life is a boring one, isn't it?"

"And it's okay to feel lost now and then," I tell him, thinking of the mess of music in my head that has no shape, that has no voice, that has no clue what it's doing. "Some people get lost ... but as it turns out, getting lost is the only way we can—"

"Find ourselves," finishes a voice from behind me.

I turn. Dmitri stands there with a knowing smirk on his full, sexy lips. He recently got a lip ring, which I find so damned sexy, I can't stand it. He really rubbed off on me, what with the new musical-note tattoo on my shoulder, and the curly spread of piano notes I'm planning for my upper back.

"Hi, Dmitri," greets Eric.

"Hey there, Eric." Dmitri slaps him on the back, then pulls him in for a big squeeze. "Is Sam finally convincing you to kick the Bail-boy to the curb? It's going to be a mighty cold curb, tonight."

"Too cold," agrees Eric, "just like last winter. No, I'll need my snuggle buddy. You know, I just need to talk to him. Real talk. Open talk. Let it all out, and let him have it all out. Though it's that second bit that scares me more than the first." He nods at the both of us, then eyes me importantly. "Thanks, Sam, for your otherworldly wisdom. *Dare to be messy!*"

"Dare to be messy," I agree, "except in the instance of leaving empty champagne glasses on the dessert table."

He swipes it back into his hand, grabs his unfinished plate of dessert, then pops the last bite of cake into his mouth with his fingers.

"Sam, I came to fetch you," announces Dmitri.

I turn to him. "What for?"

"Dessie needs you by the piano."

My fingers turn to ice at once. "I, um, what?"

Dmitri puts a gentle arm around my back. "Come, babe."

The pair of us—or, rather, trio of us, if Eric is following—cut through the crowd to the baby grand in the center of the room where Dessie, Victoria, and Victoria's beau Dirk are hanging out. At the sight of me, Dessie's face lights up.

She grabs me by the wrist and excitedly pulls me to the piano bench. "We're going to do a song!" she announces to me.

I blink. "Say what?"

"Okay, okay, okay. Remember that time when I first took you to the theater on Broadway and we got on that big old stage and you just played from your heart and I sang from mine?"

Oh dear God, no. "Dessie ..."

"We made brilliant music on the spot," she goes on, oblivious to the pulmonary embolism happening in me at her words. "It came out of nowhere. Improvised brilliance."

"That's subjective," I mumble.

"Dirk's here with his guitar. As you can obviously tell, the quartet I arranged to have here couldn't make it, hence the silence—"

"It's not silent in here," I mumble through the ceaseless chatter and laughter in the room.

"So I was thinking, as a little treat, you and Dirk could sort of ... riff off a little. Play off the cuff. Improvise." She gives the piano bench a pat, then pretty much squishes me down onto it. I comply, my weak knees no match for Dessie's pushiness. "Start it off. Dirk's already plugged in and amped and ready to jump in when he feels it."

Dirk, for emphasis, lifts his guitar. He's a spunky, slender sort of guy with messy hair—a total

90s rocker cliché with a pinch of emo, a spritz of hipster, and a modest splash of metrosexual. Victoria bites her lip and stands near him, excited to hear what we come up with.

"And you're going to sing?" I suggest, petrified so badly that I can hardly make words.

"This room's heard enough of me," says Dessie with a roll of her eyes. "A whole evening of me, in fact. It's your moment to shine." Then she leans in. "Everyone who means anything on Broadway is here tonight, so, like ... y'know. No pressure. But you're brilliant in every sense of the word, so I ain't sweatin'."

Spoken like a true Texan with those words, which makes me chuckle. Wait, no, I'm not chuckling. My mouth is frozen. Everything is frozen. The chuckle is locked away inside me, as is any capability of making my muscles work.

Dessie has to be shitting me right now.

It's either me or our positioning here around the piano, but I feel the sound in the room drain away like thick, soapy water in a bathtub, as if suddenly the room has come to expect a performance.

Fuck.

The voices damper down to nothing but hums, and I experience a very strange and terrifying tunnel vision that blurs out the whole world—except for the eighty-eight keys in front of me.

They're so ... *white*.

Blindingly white, with the black sharps and flats giving a well-needed reprieve from the glare of all that distressing ivory.

"You've got this, babe."

I glance up and find Dmitri and Eric at the other side of the piano. Dmitri is looking sexy as hell and calm as a banana. Eric is trying not to tip himself over with all the champagne making a carousel in his skull, half-clinging to Dmitri to keep upright.

Dare to be messy.

A sudden rush of flare and drama finds me. My fear shatters in an instant. I lift my chin proudly like a diva who's toured the world wide with her magnificent music that demands attention, bring my steady hands to the keys, and then strike my first chord.

The noise in the room cuts to nothing.

F major. My first chord of choice. A bold chord. A *ready* chord. It's ready to chase its way up to resolution with C, or settle downward into something curious with D.

Which way do I go?

I strike a G# major, neither of the choices I gave myself.

My eyes close.

Dare to be dirty.

I turn that chord minor, add a seventh, and then let my left hand give us a slinky bass line, playing along the deep notes like a bass guitar in a jazz club.

Where is this music coming from? I'm not even drunk.

Maybe it's my father in me after all.

I strike another chord, then start to develop a rhythm. My right hand tinkles high notes without my permission, harmonizing with the bass, and before our eyes and ears, a song takes shape.

Then, as if by the cue of a sheet of music that doesn't exist, Dirk comes right in on my next chord, anticipating it from the rhythm I've created, and he's playing a sexy riff that goes along with my tune. He even plays off of me, adding sixth and seventh notes to my every chord, jazzing it up with a pinch of spice wherever he can fit it.

Holy crap. We're making music.

And it's really, really good.

Of course, I let it get to my head right away, because why not? I purse my lips like a cocky mo-fo and add twice as much vigor to my playing, banging the keys with strength and turning up the heat on my twisting, playful, flirty chords. Whistles are returned from the room. I hear a shout from my right and a holler of excitement from my left.

My hands are ignited. My soul is possessed by the melody.

I'm literally shimmying as I play.

Like, who the actual fuck am I?

Dirk must feel my aggression (or is it passion?) because he starts jamming out on the guitar in time with my music, matching my forceful chords, and it is a beautiful marriage of rock, jazz, and something cleverly new all at once.

And in our ringing harmonies and overtones, I feel the soul of another instrument entirely, an instrument that's not here, an instrument that's playing in my memories from years, years, years ago.

I hear a bassoon.

It's singing a sweet, proud song of its own, like a surprise solo in the concerto. I don't even think it's Tomas playing the bassoon, to be honest. It's like the instrument I've always hated has sucked up a lungful of courage, and it's stepping into a room it's been told to stay out of all its life.

I'm looking at that bassoon. I'm hearing its song. I'm listening to it for once.

Dare to be daring.

That bassoon is the weirdo who no one let sit with them at the lunch tables. That bassoon is the one that's shrugged off in favor of the famous violin, or the bold piano, or the proud trumpets. That bassoon is even someone *I've* spent my whole life mocking, pushing away, feeling disgust toward, and never letting in.

That bassoon ... is me.

My music changes tone. Dirk follows like a pro. The chords turn gentle, but the bass line still flirts, pulling us through a sonic landscape of mourning, then of hope, then of wonder.

The chords are full. The music reaches its end.

And then I strike an A minor ... my right hand gliding up the notes I scratched into the wall of my garage when I was a little kid, my daddy tinkering around: A ... B ... C ... D ... E ... F ...

And then with a G, the song ends.

I lift my gaze from the keys, returning from my trance. For a second, I wonder if the whole thing was in my head and I haven't even started playing at all.

Then the room erupts into applause and cheers. Dessie has her hands to her mouth, her eyes glimmering with happiness at whatever I just unleashed from my being. Dirk is taking in the applause with humbleness, bowing his head and giving little waves to the crowds—at least until Victoria throws her arms around him and plants a big kiss on his startled face.

I turn to Dmitri and Eric, both of whom are smiling at me in awe.

And while staring at the love of my life and his old roommate, I realize how stupid lucky I am and how much time I've wasted denying myself the creative, artistic pleasure of letting in certain things … like bassoons. I'm going to put one in my newest work, which sits awaiting me in the form of digitalized noise on my laptop and a bunch of papers and notebooks on my piano at home.

The first thing I'm going to do when we all— drunken Brant and giggly Nell and cake-filled little Zara included—get back to my place is: I'm going to add a bassoon to my work.

And a hundred seventh chords.

And a minor ninth and a handful of diminished chords, too. Why not?

I'm going to mess it all up—and proudly.

Because it's good to be weird.

Clayton

It's always an interesting experience, watching a roomful of faces come to life when Samantha Hart sits at the piano and bears her soul through her powerful music.

And not being able to hear a note of it.

But boy, do I feel it. If anyone looks at Sam and thinks her to be a meek little emo girl, they'd be proven dead wrong when she's given an instrument. She commands it with such force that I literally feel the music through my feet. My chest vibrates with every bass note. My fingers tingle when Dirk hits a killer chord on his guitar. If I'm not crazy, I'd even swear that my hair is stirred by the ringing blast of music coming from that dynamic duo.

I can guarantee you, it won't be the last time they play together.

The music had interrupted Brant and I chatting. He seems to be convinced that I was let down by the fact that he and Nell declined our invitations over the years, but I was quick to assure him that it wasn't the case. He has a family now, and family always comes first.

Then he said something unexpected: "*But you're my family, too. You're the brother I never had. And you'll always—mark my fuckin' words, my fuckin' lips—you will always be my brother.*"

I damn near shed a tear at that, then pulled him in for a bone-crushing hug. Maybe literally. He hasn't quite been walking straight ever since I let him go.

Shit, I miss my best friend.

He had tried (or, rather, fumbled awkwardly) with his signs, but managed to get a few sentences going as we chatted about various grievances in our lives—his daughters' antics, his wife's antics, his parents' antics and constant meddling (they're so fucking excited to have granddaughters), and then all my stresses, my lighting designs and gigs at over seven theaters in town, and I even share a story about a sign-language-inclined lady at the sandwich place I visit for lunch every Tuesday, Thursday, and Friday. Brant couldn't seem to wipe the smile off his face as we chatted away, reminding me—even with the extra pounds he's put on both in his body and his shaggy hair—of the boy I grew up with. He even offered staying an extra day or two to take professional photos of our show—the set, the characters, a scene or two—and I told him that'd be fucking great. Dessie, in fact, was secretly hoping Brant would offer so she didn't have to be presumptuous in asking.

After Sam and Dirk's impromptu musical performance—during which Brant put Zara on his shoulders so she could watch it over everyone's heads—Brant faces me again showing an expression of awe on his face. *"That was amazing, dude. Sam has got some talent!"*

I smirk knowingly and nod. I'm so fucking glad Sam came into Dessie's life so many years ago in that fortuitous, random roommate selection process at the dormitories. Dessie lucked out, that's for sure. Not to mention having Victoria as a neighbor right across the hallway. Those three have been peas in one crazy, creative pod. Between them, they could own New York in a hot minute.

Zara starts moving her hands at me suddenly over Brant's head, still perched on his shoulders: *I want more cake.*

I laugh, watching Brant's confused face, then

sign back to her: *Ask your daddy.*

Zara's face wrinkles, then she signs: *No.*

I point at him demonstratively, then sign again: *Ask your daddy. Not me.*

She huffs: *More cake.*

I lift an eyebrow: *Daddy.*

To my utter surprise, Brant catches on and joins in with a few clumsy signs of his own: *No cake. Sugar. Awake. Bad.* Then after fumbling for a second, he speaks the rest instead: *"You are already up way past your bedtime, young lady. I'm surprised you aren't dead asleep yet, considering it's even an hour later here than it is at home."*

Zara pouts, her eyes meeting mine. I feel so much for the little girl, having taken the time to learn way more signs than she needed to for basic communication—which is what Brant and Nell apparently chose to do with all their kids. So to ease her frustration, I make a silly face at her, shoving my thumbs in my ears, sticking out my tongue, and blowing up my cheeks. Zara laughs, then says something I can't make out with her tiny lips. I make another crazy face and she laughs harder, then signs: *Fun, fun, fun, fun, fun*—over and over.

Fun, indeed. I haven't had this much fucking

fun in so long.

Feeling a presence near me suddenly, I turn. Dessie stands there with her hands clasped. She was watching me being silly with Zara, though I can't say for how long. There's a curious sparkle in her eyes, the sparkle of thoughts and wonders and dreams.

I lean in and give Dessie a kiss, then pull back. "Sam's got quite a set of hands for that piano."

She smiles. *As always*—she signs, the strangely wistful look in her eyes still there.

I frown slightly, then lift my hands: *What's wrong?*

Dessie shakes her head—*Nothing*—then puts an arm around my waist and, with one hand, signs what she's saying to Brant: "*Sam and Dmitri are about to head back and wanted to know if you and Nell want to come with them, or stay longer.*"

Brant pats the legs of his little one still on his shoulders, then says, "*We need to get the little one to bed. We should go. I had a great time. Thanks for having us, and congrats on your show.*"

I caught every word, since Brant's lips were particularly expressive—likely because he's having to shout over the noise in the room. Dessie signs her

response again for my benefit as she speaks it: "*I'm really glad you two came. It was a pleasant surprise. We need to do a lot of hanging out and catching up over the weekend while you're in town.*"

With that, Brant gives Dessie a hug, then crouches down slightly so Dessie can give her own little goodbye to Zara, who signs—*Cake, fun, cake, fun*—over and over, then waves bye at both of us as the pair of them disappear into the crowd seeking Nell and the others.

Over the course of another hour or two, the room slowly clears out, and soon, Dessie and I and a couple stragglers are the only ones left other than Dessie's parents and Celia—Dessie's sister—who are helping put away and package up the leftover desserts with the hired help. The strangers seem too drunk to function, or else they're waiting on their cabs, if I had to guess.

Dessie tugs on my hand, then draws me off to the half-lit den, away from the main hall. A gloriously tall, ornate window that touches the floor stretches by our side, overlooking the city and the pale moonlight.

Before I can ask her what's on her mind, she kisses me, then tucks her fingers into the pockets of my fitted jeans and pulls my hips against hers. I breathe in deeply, consumed by her vigorous kiss. She smells so inviting.

When we pull apart, my eyes meet hers, and I lift my brows, curious.

She starts moving her hands: *You know how much I love you, right?*

I lift a corner of my lips, amused: *Most of the time,* I sign back teasingly.

Dessie bites her lip: *I would do anything for you, and make any sacrifice for you ... just to show that I love you. To prove to you.*

Now my lightness is eclipsed by a knobby branch of doubt, casting a shadow over my face. I frown and lift my hands: *What's going on?*

I love you—she signs again.

Should I be worried? I lift my hands again: *I love you, too. Now tell me what the fuck is going on.* I swallow hard, then add: *Please.*

Dessie presses her lips together, then moves away from me and sits on the arm of the fancy couch that stretches half the length of the room. Her face is beautifully lit half in moonlight, half in the warm amber light from an decorative glass lamp in the corner of the room.

Then she signs to me: *I saw you interacting with Brant's daughter.*

I nod, then gesture a hand, encouraging her to keep explaining.

She does: *It breaks my heart to think I'm denying you the chance to have one of your own.*

And now we've reached her point. Softer now, I move to her and sit right by her, then slip an arm around the back of her waist, pulling her against my body. After putting a kiss on her pretty head of hair, I use my voice: *"Baby, you're not denying me a thing."*

She signs with her hands barely hovered out of her lap: *It doesn't feel like I'm not. The only reason we haven't tried is because of my career. I know you have the desire to have a family. You want little ones someday. My parents can be grandparents. Yours.*

I smirk. "My messed-up parents can go right to Hell with their grams-and-gramps wishes."

She turns slightly, looking up into my eyes. Then she moves her lips.

It's been so long since I've read her lips, as we tend to only sign lately, that it catches me by surprise. I miss all her words, so hypnotized by the way her sexy mouth moves. "What?" I hum.

She smiles, then repeats herself: *"I'm saying I*

want to have your child."

I watch her for a long while, unable to pull my gaze from her beautiful face. Is she serious? This is truly what she wants? "You?" I murmur, lifting my eyebrows. "You want this? You want a baby?"

She nods slowly, then puts a hand on my thigh as she says, "*I want to have a little Dessie or Clayton. I want us to have that.*"

My whole world changes in the space of a kiss, a glance in her eyes, and a reading of her lips.

She wants a child.

I'd abandoned this very possibility for so long, caught up in our careers as we've been. We haven't so much as tapped the brake pedals all these years. We've been so busy building a life for ourselves that the mere *chance* of including someone else in that life—some *little* someone else—never even crossed my mind.

Well, not until I got a look at that cute little Zara and watched her moving her tiny hands at me, making words, speaking to me without sound. Maybe I always thought I'd be a failure of a dad because of my own. Or because of my ears. Or because of a hundred other reasons.

A hundred reasons to say *no* to becoming a dad.

Maybe I just needed one reason to say yes.

"I love you, Dessie," I tell the love of my life with my words, bringing both my arms around her slender, beautiful, supple body. "And I've always been fairly certain that there would never be anyone else in this world I could possibly love as much as I love you ... until now."

Dessie lifts her pretty face to mine, her lips parted. "*And who's that?*"

I bring my lips to hers, tasting her deeply, then pull away to answer her: "The baby we're about to make."

Then with a sweep of our bodies, Dessie is in my arms, and she lets out a yelp of surprise that quickly melts into joyous laughter. I can almost truly hear the laughter as it pours from her beautiful lips, her arms clinging to my body as I carry my wife off to start ourselves a family. I often dream of what her laughter might sound like, had I the gift of hearing for just one second, for just one fleeting, perfect moment ... to hear my love, Desdemona Lebeau-Watts, as she laughs so happily.

I bet it sounds like music.

· *The End* ·

25430266R00065

Made in the USA
Columbia, SC
04 September 2018